Miss Bindergarten Plans a Circus

with Kindergarten

by JOSEPH SLATE

illustrated by ASHLEY WOLFF

Dutton Children's Books · New York

For Anna, Ben, Colleen, Emma, Erin, Jacob,
John Edward, Kate, Keara, Sarah, Sean,
Tessa, and Zach—bring on the clowns

J.S.

To Barbara Fong—a talented and generous teacher

A.W.

Text copyright © 2002 by Joseph Slate
Illustrations copyright © 2002 by Ashley Wolff

CIP Data is available.

Published in the United States by Dutton Children's Books,
a division of Penguin Putnam Books for Young Readers
345 Hudson Street, New York, New York 10014
www.penguinputnam.com
First Edition   Printed in USA
ISBN 0-525-46884-6
2 4 6 8 10 9 7 5 3 1

"There's much to do," says Miss B,
"to make this circus fun to see."

Adam Krupp is all keyed up.
Brenda says, "Way cool!"

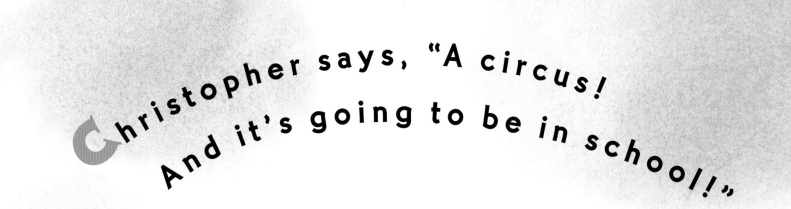

Christopher says, "A circus! And it's going to be in school!"

with kindergarten.

Danny paints a poster.

Emily's got BIG feet.

Franny numbers tickets to match each fold-up seat.

Miss Bindergarten plans a circus

with kindergarten.

Gwen turns seven somersaults.

Henry hula-hoops.

Ian is so nervous that his stomach loops-the-loop.

Miss Bindergarten plans a circus

with kindergarten.

Jessie shapes pink popcorn balls.

Kiki stirs limeade.

Lenny wraps red ribbons to lead the big parade.

Miss Bindergarten plans a circus

with kindergarten.

Matty tips his top hat.

Noah rips his tights.

Ophelia helps her mom and dad untangle colored lights.

Miss Bindergarten plans— **OOPS!**

—a circus with kindergarten.

Patricia is a blue Bo-Peep.

Quentin lifts a ton.

Raffie and **S**ara sneak a peek to see just who has come.

The planning is all done.

The **CIRCUS** has begun.

Tommy dares a daunting dive.

Ursula is a star.

Vicky jumps like a jack-in-the-box from a jazzy purple car.

Wanda twirls a green baton.

Xavier rolls a tire.

Yolanda follows **Z**ach across the wob-b-b-ly "high wire."

"Ladies and gents," says Matty,
"we hope you've had some fun.
But we *still* have a treat,
so don't leave your seat

till you've seen the act to come.
And now . . .
presenting the great—
I bet you can't wait—

Matty whoops and hurls his hat.
"Let's hear a cheer right now
for Miss Bindergarten
and her kindergarten
as they take a
final bow."

We love CIRCUS colors!

Noah's top is red.

Patricia's dress is blue.

Ian's broom is yellow.

Raffie's pants have orange stripes.

Ophelia's shirt is green.

Jessie's wig is purple.

Sara's wig is pink.

Christopher's fur is gray.

Brenda's fur is brown.

Matty's hat is black.

Yellow + Red = Orange

Red + Blue = Purple

Blue + Yellow = Green

Red
Orange
Yellow
Green
Blue
Indigo
Violet

The colors of the rainbow.

Adam · **A**lligator

Brenda · **B**eaver

Christopher · **C**at

Danny · **D**og

Emily · **E**lephant

Franny · **F**rog

Gwen · **G**orilla

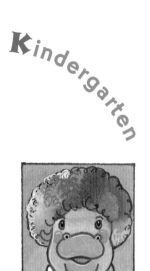

Henry · **H**ippopotamus

Ian · **I**guana

Jessie · **J**aguar

Kiki · **K**angaroo

Lenny · **L**ion

Matty · **M**oose

Noah · **N**ewt

Ophelia · **O**tter

Patricia · **P**ig

Quentin · **Q**uokka

Raffie · **R**hinoceros

Sara · **S**quirrel

Tommy · **T**iger

Ursula · **U**akari monkey

Vicky · **V**ole

Wanda · **W**olf

Xavier · **X**enosaurus

Yolanda · **Y**ak

Zach · **Z**ebra

Coco · **C**ockatoo